DETECTIVE Zack

Secrets in the Sand

Written by
Jerry D. Thomas

Illustrated by
Lad Odell

A Faith Building Guide can be found on page 127.

Faith Building Guide

Ages
9 and up

Trust

Faith Kids® is an imprint of
Cook Communications Ministries, Colorado Springs, CO 80918
Cook Communications, Paris, Ontario
Kingsway Communications, Eastbourne, England

DETECTIVE ZACK: THE SECRETS IN THE SAND
© 2002 by Jerry D. Thomas

First Printing, 1992 (Pacific Press)
First Faith Kids® Printing, 2002
Printed in the United States of America
1 2 3 4 5 6 7 8 9 10 Printing/Year 06 05 04 03 02

Edited by: Heather Gemmen
Designed by: Big Mouth Bass Design, Inc.
Cover Illustrated by: Lad Odell

Library of Congress Cataloging-in-Publication Data

Thomas, Jerry D., 1959-
    Detective Zack: secrets in the sand / written by Jerry D.
Thomas ; illustrated by Lad Odell.
        p. cm. -- (Detective Zack ; 4)
    Summary: On a trip through the Middle East, ten-year-old Zack is
introduced to archaeological and other evidence that supports the
reliability of historical sections of the Bible.
    ISBN 0-7814-3803-9
    [1. Bible--Antiquities--Fiction. 2. Archaeology--Fiction. 3.
Christian life--Fiction.]   I. Odell, Lad, ill. II. Title. III.
Series: Thomas, Jerry D., 1959-   . Detective Zack ; v 4.
    PZ7.T366954 Dgk 2002
    [Fic]--dc21
                                    2001004332

Dedication

To my parents,
Hagar and Jean Thomas,
who have always believed in me.
Looks like it's Sydney!

Note to Parents and Teachers

The archeological information in this book is accurate, but it is not intended to be precise or complete. It is intended to be simple enough for young minds to understand.

Also, the sequence of sites visited on this trip may not follow the normal, logical route of a common tourist. Instead, the sites and experiences are arranged in such a way as to appeal to the logic and interest of young minds intent on following their heroes of the Bible.

Books in this Series

(1)   Detective Zack: Secret of Noah's Flood

(2)   Detective Zack: Mystery at Thunder Mountain

(3)   Detective Zack: Danger at Dinosaur Camp

(4)   Detective Zack: Secrets in the Sand

(5)   Detective Zack: Red Hat Mystery

(6)   Detective Zack: Missing Manger Mystery

Contents

1 Detective Zack Is Back!   7

2 A Long Time Ago   15

3 Big Tents, Big Towers   27

4 Secret Codes and Camels   37

5 Friends that Rhyme   47

6 Danger in the Dust   57

7 Buried Treasure   67

8 Abraham's Picnic   75

9 Old Beauty   85

10 Three Sheep and a Bowl of Beans   93

11 Deep Trouble   101

12 A Really Big Watchdog?   109

13 Secrets in the Sand   119

   Faith Building Guide   127

ONE

Detective Zack Is Back!

Unexpected Adventure

Did you know that from the top, clouds look like the whipped cream on a strawberry shortcake? Well, the ones I'm looking at do. Sometimes I can see down to the blue ocean and sometimes I can only see white.

I guess you have figured out that I'm on a jet airplane. It's going to be a long ride—all day and all night. So I have plenty of time to explain what case I'm on this time and where I'm going.

This adventure really started when we were watching a TV show. It was a hot, lazy, end-of-the-summer evening. Mom made popcorn and we each grabbed a root beer and sat down to watch "Walking on Water Buffalo: the Life of a Cattle Egret" or something like that. When it was over, I swallowed the last drops of my root beer while Kayla and Alex, my little sister and brother, argued over who had to get in the tub first.

Mom and Dad were sitting on the couch, talking seriously and quietly about something important. I thought it probably had something to do with my dad's trip. I knew he was going to some other country for a few weeks. But since he was leaving at the same time that school was starting, I knew that I wasn't going. So I really wasn't paying much attention.

Then a voice from the TV spoke up. "*Myths and Legends.* This week, we look at two popular characters from the Bible. We'll see how the mythical stories of Abraham and Moses were created to give the ancient Hebrew people history and heroes."

I looked at Dad. He looked at Mom. Alex looked at me and asked, "What does mythical mean?" He's only seven so he doesn't know these things.

"*Mythical* means pretend or made up. Myths are stories made up about people who didn't really live. But the people are usually heroes. Kind of like Superman or Santa Claus or Paul Bunyan," I explained.

Alex was confused. He turned back to Mom and Dad. "But you told us that Abraham and Moses were real people, not pretend like Santa Claus."

"That's right, Alex," Dad said. "They really did live just like you and me. But it was a long time ago."

"That's not what the man on TV said," I pointed out. "He said that Abraham and Moses were mythical people"

"Well, he's wrong," Mom replied.

"How do we know? Is there any evidence that Bible people like Moses and Abraham really lived?" I asked.

Dad looked at Mom. She looked at me and squinted her eyes. Then she turned back to Dad. "Okay. You're right. He should go with you."

Now that got my attention. "He's right about what? Go where? What are you talking about?"

Dad laughed. "Stop talking so I can tell you."

I took a deep breath.

"Zack, you're going with me. I'm going on this trip to find evidence about the people in the Bible, so you're going with me."

I jumped up. "Alright!" Then I thought more. "Wait a minute. Where are we going? And what about school?"

"You'll have to miss a few weeks of school," Mom said. "I don't know what your principal will say."

"It'll be alright," Dad said. "You can catch up. You'll learn more on this trip than you would in school anyway."

I looked at both of them. They just stared back at me. Kayla and Alex were staring at me too.

"Well?" I asked.

"Well what?" Dad acted confused, but he was laughing.

"Where are we going?" I almost yelled.

Dad finally told. "We're going across the ocean to the Middle East, to Egypt and Israel. And you, Detective Zack, are going to track down the people of the old Bible days. You're going to search for evidence that the people in the Bible were real and that the Bible stories are true."

I just stood there with my mouth open.

"Zack? What do you think? Do you want to go?" Mom looked worried as she spoke. "I'm not sure he wants to go," she said to my dad. She put her hand on my forehead. "It's all right, dear. You can stay here."

I pushed her hand away. "No, no, I'm going. To Egypt, really? And see the pyramids? And the Nile River with the crocodiles?"

Dad grinned. "That's right, Zack."

"And to Israel? And see Jericho and Jerusalem and the place where David fought Goliath?" I asked.

"Yes, yes," Dad said. "That's where we're going. Soon."

"Hey." Kayla was standing up beside me now. "What about me? I want to go too."

"I'm sorry, sweetheart, but I can't take you," Dad said as he knelt down beside her. "I wish everyone could go. But it's just not possible. It's just too expensive."

Alex walked over next to Dad. "I want to go with you, Daddy," he said with tears in his eyes.

By then I was starting to feel kind of bad for them. I knew that I wouldn't have wanted to be the one to stay home. Dad put his arms around both of them.

"I want to take you. But I can't."

"But how come Zack gets to go?" Kayla asked.

Dad pushed her brown hair back out of her eyes. "I love all of the you the same, Kayla, but I can't treat you all the same all the time. Zack is older than you and you are older than Alex. Some things you'll get to do and the boys won't. Some things they'll get to do and you won't. This is one of those things."

Mom stepped in quickly. "Besides, I need you both here with me. We're going to do some special things here."

Alex still wasn't happy. "Aw, nothing is as neat as crocodiles and David and Goliath."

"Well, I don't know. Grandma is coming to stay with us for two weeks."

"Really? Oh, boy!" Kayla smiled at that idea.

Mom smiled too. "Really. And Alex, you wouldn't want to miss your day of first grade."

"Oh, yeah! I almost forgot."

Soon they were having a regular huddle about their plans. Dad and I walked over to the kitchen table and talked about the trip.

"Zack, I want you to come with me on this trip because I think you can learn a lot. But it's not going to be an easy trip. We're going to be traveling every day and sometimes it will be very hot and crowded. I'm not even sure where we'll sleep every night."

I didn't care about that. "Who are we going with?"

Dad explained. "I've been planning to go on this trip with an old friend of mine, Dr. Doone. He's an archeologist. You remember what an archeologist is, don't you?"

I remembered. "An archeologist studies things from

long ago. He digs up bones and old bowls and spears."

"Right. And since the people of the Bible lived long ago, archeologists have been digging in Israel and Egypt and all over that part of the world."

"Is Dr. Doone going back there to dig in some of those places?" I asked.

"Not this time. He's going to film a video about archeology and famous Bible places and people. He invited me along to help with the camera. I'm bringing you to help me and to see these things for yourself."

That sounded like a lot of fun. "Alright, Dad. That'll be great. But I'll need a new notebook."

"Alright, Detective Zack. I'll get you a brand new notebook. I want you to keep track of all the evidence we see, just like last time."

He was talking about the trip we took last summer. We searched for evidence that Noah's Flood really happened. And we found it! But that's another story.

So now you know why I'm on this plane going halfway around the world. I hope we find the clues we're looking for. We're going to need them. Let me tell you what happened while we were waiting at the airport.

This lady asked where we were going. Dad told her about the video and archeology and people of the Bible. She laughed right in his face! Then...oops, I have to put this away for now. The flight attendants are serving our dinner now. I wonder what airplane food tastes like?

Discoveries and Clues

Words to Remember

Evidence: Clues detectives use to prove that something really happened or didn't happen

Archeology: Study of things from the past—bones, pottery, bricks, anything that tells something about people who lived long ago

Myths, Legends: Made-up stories from long ago that didn't really happen but are told to explain history or to make heroes

Important Facts

A lot of people believe that the Bible stories never really happened, that the people are just made up like other mythical characters.

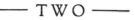

TWO

A Long Time Ago

A Colorful Past

The clouds look flatter now, kind of like marshmallow creme after you spread it on your bread for a peanut butter and marshmallow sandwich. Just looking at them makes me hungry. I know I just ate but, believe me, that meal was not worth the trip! It was little tiny servings of stuff that even my mother wouldn't make me eat.

Anyway, I was telling you about that lady at the airport. When Dad told her why we were going on this trip, she laughed.

"You still believe in those Bible stories? I thought everyone knew that they didn't really happen. The experts say that most of the Old Testament is just stories and legends people told to their children."

I looked at Dad. He just shrugged his shoulders and said, "We believe the stories are a record of real life and real people. And we're going to find evidence that proves it."

"Good luck," she laughed. "If you ask me, you'd be better off looking for evidence that Santa Claus really does live at the North Pole."

I didn't like that at all. She walked away and Dad looked at me. "Now that's a good reason to go on this trip, don't you think?"

You can be sure that I'm writing down every bit of evidence we find. I hope there's a lot of it.

Dad and I met up with Dr. Doone in New York City. I saw the Statue of Liberty from the airplane window, but we didn't have time to visit it. Maybe on the next trip.

Just watching the topsides of clouds can get boring. It's been kind of a bumpy flight and I'm too wound up to sleep. Not Dad, though. He spent the last hour snoring into his pillow against the window on the other side of the plane. And I'm still hungry.

I was just trying to figure out where they might be hiding the peanut butter on this plane when Dr. Doone came over to talk. He's really neat. He's been to the Bible lands lots of times and has lots of stories to tell. And he knows everything about archeology. Well, almost everything.

"No one knows everything about archeology, Zack," he told me. "You can't be completely sure about most things. At an archeological site, called a *dig*, we might find a piece of pottery, a broken brick, or what was left of a wall."

"That's all? What can you tell by those things?" I asked.

"Sometimes, not very much. It's like trying to put together a few pieces of a jigsaw puzzle and guessing what the picture is supposed to be."

"Why don't you find more? One time I dug in a trash pit behind an old house and found bottles and cans and an old newspaper from 1903."

"Wow. 1903? That was a long time ago. You're very lucky that the newspaper was still in one piece."

I nodded at him. "I know it was a long time ago. Dad said that in 1903, my great-grandfather was just a boy."

Dr. Doone smiled. "That was almost a hundred years ago. But archeologists study things even older than that. Do you know when the United States fought the Revolutionary War and became a free country?"

"Sure I do. In 1776, on July 4th. That's why we celebrate the Fourth of July, with fireworks and everything."

"And that was more than 200 years ago," Dr. Doone said. "But what about before that? Do you know when Columbus discovered America?"

I had to think about that. Then I remembered,

Columbus sailed the ocean blue
in fourteen hundred ninety-two.

"Fourteen ninety-two," I said.

"And how long ago was that?" he asked.

Ow! It almost hurt to think that hard. "It was…more than 500 years ago!" I guess I said it too loud. The people sitting in front of us turned around. Then a flight attendant stopped at our row.

"Did you need something?" she asked.

Dr. Doone laughed and looked at me. "Zack? Want anything?"

I didn't even have to think about it. "Do you have any peanut butter? I could use a sandwich."

"No, I'm sorry, we don't," she said. "But how about some peanuts?"

"Close enough," I said. "That would be great."

"And two root beers, please," Dr. Doone added.

She poured our drinks into cups and handed them over with two little bags of peanuts. I guess all food on airplanes comes in bite sizes. Luckily, Dr. Doone insisted that I eat both bags of peanuts. But just as I was opening the first one, the plane hit a bump or something and I spilled a little root beer on Dr. Doone's sleeve.

"Sorry," I said.

"No problem," he said as he wiped it with a napkin.

"Zack, do you know when Jesus lived on this earth?"

I knew it was a long time ago, but I had never heard anyone explain exactly when. Well, Dr. Doone had the answer.

"The people who made the calendar we use today, with twelve months and all, built it around Jesus. They wanted the calendar to start at the time that Jesus was here. So Jesus lived one thousand four hundred and ninety-two years before Columbus."

Now that was a long time ago. Before I could ask him more, the plane hit another bump and he spilled some of his drink. Not me, though. My cup was nearly empty.

"If the calendar is planned from when Jesus was alive, what about people who lived before Jesus? Like Daniel?" Dr. Doone drank up the rest of his root beer before he answered. "They started counting backward. Daniel lived about 500 years before Jesus did. We call that year 500 B.C. If you count back further, to the time of King David, it was about 1000 B.C."

"What does the B.C. stand for? Before calendar?"

"Not exactly," Dr. Doone said, "but that's what it means. And the years keep counting back. Moses was in Egypt around 1500 B.C. and Abraham was alive about 500 years before that, around 2000 B.C."

"That's too long ago to even imagine," I said.

"Let's see if this helps." He pulled a piece of string about two feet long out of his pocket and tied a big knot right in the middle. "Now," he said, "this rope is going to help us tell time."

"Can't we use our watches?" I asked.

"No. This is going to tell us a lot more about time than your watch could. First we need more knots." He tied small knots about two inches apart along the rest of the string, so it had four small knots, then the big one, then four more small ones.

Holding the string up by one end, he said, "Now, each small knot stands for 500 years. Let's start at the top." He reached into his coat pocket and pulled out a yellow marker. Then he colored the knot at the top of the string yellow.

"The yellow knot is today, okay? Now what happened about 500 years ago?"

"Columbus discovered America."

"Okay, we'll color that one blue." He colored it. "Now we'll skip the next two. A lot of things happened then, but we'll skip them for now. Now we'll color the big one red. It stands for the time when Jesus was here."

"You mean that America's independence and my great grandfather and everything happened between the blue knot and the yellow one? Wow." I ran my fingers along the string past the next two knots. "And Jesus lived all the way down here."

Dr. Doone went on. "Daniel's time was 500 years before Jesus. We'll color that knot…"

"Purple," I said.

"Right. Purple." He pulled out the marker and marked it. "Then when we back up another 500 years, we find King David. We'll color that one," he fumbled in his pocket, "brown. Then 500 years before David is Moses. We'll color Moses' knot…well, what about pink?"

I laughed. "I'm sure Moses would like it."

"And the last knot, 500 years before Moses, is Abraham. We'll color it black. Now, does that help you see how long ago it was?"

I held the string up and looked from the yellow knot on top down to the black one at the bottom. "Everything happened a lot longer ago than I thought."

"You keep the string, Zack. We'll need it to remind us when the people we're looking for were alive."

It was a lot to think about. I wasn't sure my brain could handle that many years. "No wonder you don't find much at your digs. It all happened too long ago. All the stuff would be rotted away."

"But that's what makes it so much fun," he said. "Every dig is like a mystery to solve with just a few clues.

Many secrets are in the sand. God used sand to cover and save some amazing things."

Later I was looking out the window, watching the clouds turn red like the sunset behind us and thinking about the thousands of years that had gone by. Suddenly an all night plane ride didn't seem like such a long trip! And I wondered, could there really be any evidence of Bible people when they lived so long ago?

I finally went to sleep sometime in the night and was nearly awake when we piled out into the airport. Dr. Doone had us loaded up in a taxi and on our way as quick as a flash. Too quick to grab anything to eat, I might add.

"Tonight we're staying with an old friend of mine," he said. "He's going to teach us something about Abraham."

We spent most of the morning speeding along dusty roads in the old taxi. The driver seemed to think we were in a race with someone. If parts of this are hard to read it's because I was bouncing off the ceiling while I wrote.

We did stop for lunch, and while the food was different than Mom's, it was very good. Much better than the airplane food. I really liked the bread. All it needed was a little peanut butter.

After lunch, Dr. Doone kept asking the driver to stop at every town. I looked over at Dad. He looked hot and dusty just like me. But he was smiling. I scooted over next to him when Dr. Doone got out at our third stop.

"Why do we keep stopping to ask where this person is?" I asked. "I thought Dr. Doone knew him."

"I'm sure he knows what he's doing. I think he has a surprise for us," Dad said.

This time, Dr. Doone came back looking happy. "Almost there. Just over a few hills."

"Are you sure?" I asked as he squeezed in the door. "This guy seems very hard to find. He must move around a lot."

"You're exactly right, Zack," he said with a roar of laughter. But he wouldn't say any more.

I saw several small hills or mounds in the distance as we drove but before I could ask about them, we bumped over the top of a big hill and Dr. Doone said, "Here we are."

All I could do was stare. In front of us were three big tents. They weren't green or blue or red like our tents. These were made of some kind of hairy-looking cloth. And I mean, these tents were big. The largest one covered more ground than our house!

And instead of a garage with a car, the only thing parked out in front was a row of camels. The back yard seemed to be mostly sheep and a few goats.

I'm sure my mouth was still hanging open when we pulled up to the big tent in a flurry of dust.

"Well, Zack? What do you think? Does it look like home?" Dr. Doone had waited all day to spring this surprise on me. I wanted to tell him it was a good trick, but all I could do was stare.

Discoveries and Clues

Words to Remember

Dig: A place where archeologists are digging and looking for clues about the past

B.C.: All the years before Jesus was here on earth

P.B.: Peanut butter—I wish I had some.

Important Facts

Everything in the Bible happened a very long time ago. I'll be surprised if we find many clues.

Archeology is like trying to solve a mystery with only a few clues.

THREE

Big Tents, Big Towers

Threat of Marriage

This morning was the first time I've ever been woken up by a herd of goats and sheep. They were right outside the tent wall bawling and bleating before the sun was even up.

Like I was telling you yesterday, we pulled up to the tents in a cloud of dust. Quickly, a tall man in a white, flowing robe stepped out. His head was covered with a white cloth headdress, just like you see on TV. Dr. Doone hopped out and greeted him.

"Sheik (shake) Hamadi, I have returned."

"How good to see you again, my friend. You are back to make your film?" the man asked with a smile. "And these are your assistants?"

Dr. Doone introduced Dad and then turned to me. "This is Zack. He wants to learn about archeology and your land."

"Welcome Zack. I'm sure you are hungry after your trip. I will rush those who are preparing food." He clapped his hands and headed into the tent. Other people in robes began scurrying around.

Dr. Doone looked at me with a big grin. "Well, Zack, what do you think?"

"What is a sheik? Does he really live here? Are they just camping out or something?" I looked over at the camels and shook my head.

Dr. Doone seemed to like my questions. "These people call the chief of their tribe a sheik. And no, they don't always live here. They always live in these tents, though. This is a tribe of Bedouin (bed-o-win) shepherds who move around the countryside with their flocks of sheep and goats. That's why I wasn't sure where to find them. They move every few months."

"Really?"

"Yes. They live very much like Abraham did when he was living in this same area long ago."

We carried our things into the tents and joined the Bedouins for their meal. It was kind of strange but I was hungry and thirsty. While I was eating a gourd-thing, I saw a face peeking around one of the curtains of the tent. It was a girl who looked about my age. The sheik saw her too.

"Ah, Zack, you see I have a child as curious as you are. Her name is Hallah. Perhaps you would like to stay with us and take her for a bride. You could become a sheik like me!" He laughed so loud the sheep outside started bleating again.

Dad was laughing too. "Zack, your face is so red, it would glow in the dark," he said. I don't know if the girl was as embarrassed as I was. All I know is that she and her face disappeared.

I found out that Bedouins go to sleep when it gets dark. It's easy to understand why. It's not like they could stay up and watch TV or ride a camel into town for an ice cream.

Early this morning, Dr. Doone and Dad set up the camera to film the shepherds and their flocks. I helped them get the cables all connected and the floodlights in place. Dad looked through the camera and adjusted the lights until they were ready.

"Okay, go," he said.

Dr. Doone began to speak as the shepherds and sheep moved past him. "Abraham's shepherds began their day driving their flocks to pasture, just as these shepherds are doing. Just like this Bedouin sheik, the tribal chief of today, Abraham's wealth was calculated by the size of his flocks—the number of sheep, goats, and camels that he owned."

I watched the animals go by as Dr. Doone talked. I noticed that Hallah, the sheik's daughter, was herding the sheep, too. When she saw me looking at her, she waved. Of course I had to wave back. Americans are supposed to be friendly, right?

Later, I helped Dad load the cameras and stuff into the taxi for a trip. As we pulled away in a dust cloud, I asked Dr. Doone where we were going. "We're going to a place near Hebron where we know Abraham really lived."

After today, I can tell you what it would be like to get sucked up inside a vacuum cleaner—you'd be bouncing off the sides and dust would be everywhere. That's exactly how I felt in that taxi. But since we were trapped there, I whipped out my notebook and asked Dr. Doone to tell me more about Abraham. Of course, my writing will look like chicken scratches.

"Alright, Doctor, I need some facts. What evidence is there that Abraham really lived here like our friends, the Bedouins?"

"Well, Zack, let's start at the beginning. Where does the Bible say Abraham was from?"

I reached in my duffel bag for my Bible. "Look in Genesis 11:31," he said.

I bounced off the ceiling twice before I found it. "From...Ur? What kind of name is *Ur?*"

He laughed as he reached out to catch a box that was trying to bounce out the window. "Ur was a very important city in Abraham's day. Archeologists have uncovered the old city of Ur in Iraq, about 100 miles from the Persian Gulf."

"Whoa," I said, "isn't that where they had the Persian Gulf War?"

"Yes: Operation Desert Storm. But archeologists worked there for many years before that. It's easy to see why the Bible's story of Abraham begins there. In fact, that's a clue for you to write down, Zack. According to archeologists, the oldest cities in the world, the ones built before any others, are in that area. That whole area is called Mesopotamia (mess-o-po-tame-e-uh)."

"So what's the clue?"

"Well, according to the Bible, where should we find the oldest cities?"

I thought about that. I knew the Flood during Noah's time had destroyed everything built since Adam and Eve. Where did people live after that? What story comes after the story of the Flood? The car spun a little to the left and I slid toward the door. Then it hit me. No, not the door, the answer.

"The Tower of Babel!" I exclaimed. This puzzle was coming together. "After the Flood, people tried to build a tower high enough to reach heaven. So the oldest cities should be there."

"Exactly right," Dr. Doone said. "And where does the Bible say that tower was built?"

I looked it up. "In the land of Babylonia."

"And guess what city is just up the road from Ur?"

"Babylon!"

"That's right. The Hebrew people sometimes called the land of Babylon by a different name: Shinar. But Babylon—or Shinar—is the place where the Tower of Babel was built. The people of that land built many towers, not just the one we know about. They called the towers *ziggurats* (zig-er-ots). The name *ziggurat* means 'stairway to heaven.'"

"Just like the story in the Bible," I said. "This is good evidence that the stories in the Bible are real."

"In fact," Dr. Doone said, "we have found the remains of many towers in that area. And lots of artifacts (are-tih-fax). That's what we call the things we dig up from an old city or site."

"Wait a minute," I said, brushing a fly away from my ear. "What about the big one? The Tower of

Babel. Have archeologists found that?"

"Maybe. Near Babylon they found the remains of a foundation, the underground base, of a giant ziggurat. It might have been the Tower of Babel. But better than that, archeologists have found copies of a poem that talks about a time when everyone spoke the same language. Then something happened and people started talking different languages."

"Hey," I said, "that sounds just like the Tower of Babel story in the Bible. But I thought stuff like paper didn't last very long before it rotted away and turned into dust. How did they find something like that poem written down?"

That's when it happened. The taxi stopped and smoke started pouring out from under the hood. We piled out onto the sand to look.

"What happened?" Dad asked the driver.

"The engine, she is burned up," he answered after peering into the black smoke for a little while. "A town is near. I will find another ride." With that, he stepped quickly across the sand and soon disappeared over the next hill.

I looked at Dad. He shrugged his shoulders. "If we're going to wait, it might as well be in the shade," he said as he sat down in the small shadow of the car.

"Dad," I asked as I slid down beside him, "how hot is it out here?"

"Oh, 105, 110 degrees, maybe."

I sure hope that driver comes back soon.

Discoveries and Clues

Words to Remember

Bedouins: A tribe of shepherds who live in tents and move around the countryside to find grass for their flocks of sheep

Sheik: Chief of a tribe of Bedouin shepherds

Hallah: Trouble (at least that's *my* definition)

Artifacts: Things dug up from old cities and sites, including bowls, swords, tablets, bricks, and lots of other stuff

Ziggurat: A tower made like a giant staircase

Important Facts

The Bedouin shepherds still live a lot like the Bible says Abraham did.

According to the Bible, the world's oldest cities should be in the land of Babylon. According to archeologists, that's where they are found.

A poem found in the Babylon area sounds a lot like the Bible story of the Tower of Babel when God confused people's languages.

FOUR

Secret Codes and Camels

Half Baked

I'm glad it cools off quickly at night here—it was a long, hot day. Lying here on my stomach, I can see the shepherds herding those noisy sheep and goats into their pens. They make almost as much noise at night as they do in the morning. You don't need a rooster—or an alarm clock—to know its time to get up.

The sunlight is disappearing from the sky and it's getting harder to see what I'm writing, so I'd better hurry and tell you what happened.

We were sitting in the skinny shade of the car, waiting for the driver to return. I was sweating like a glass of ice water in the sun. Dr. Doone looked almost happy. He leaned back and relaxed, like he was floating in the deep end of a hotel pool.

"Aren't we lucky, Zack? Now we have time to finish talking about archeology."

"Lucky! If we get any luckier, we're gonna be French toast!" I said.

He laughed. "Now, what was it you were asking me when the car broke down? Something about the poem about Babylon…"

"Not about the poem," I said, wiping my forehead to keep the sweat from dripping in my eyes. "About the paper. How could the paper it was written on last that long?"

Dr. Doone didn't even look hot. "Very simple, Zack. It wasn't written on paper. Paper wasn't invented yet. They wrote on clay tablets. They used a tool to make kind of triangular-shaped marks on soft clay. This triangular-shaped writing is called cuneiform (q-knee-a-form), and at first no one could read it."

"Kind of like a secret code, I guess."

"Right! But archeologists finally figured it out. Then they began to learn what life was like when Abraham was alive. You know, way down at the black knot on your string."

I pulled the string out and looked at it again. "Wow! And these clay tablets lasted all the way to today?"

"Yes," he said. "When the clay is baked by fire, it becomes as hard as rock. And since many of these were buried underground, they were safely kept from being broken."

I was curious about these clay tablets. "What kind of things did they write down? Homework?" I was just joking.

"Actually, yes. Some clay tablets were used to teach people to write. You can tell where students have practiced their funny-looking letters. But mostly they've found everyday kinds of writing, like a list of everything in a rich person's storage barn. And important announcements of kings or rulers.

"Then, some archeologists uncovered the palace of a king at an ancient city called Nuzi. And this king had collected stories from all over his kingdom. He had a whole library full of clay tablets!"

"Full of stories?"

"There were stories and lists and records from all over Mesopotamia. And many of them came from the years before Abraham, before the black knot on your string. One of these stories in that library is called the Legend of Gilgamesh (gill-guh-mesh)."

"Gilga-who?"

"Gilgamesh. He told a whole book of stories, including one where the hero builds a big boat to save himself and many animals from a big flood."

"Wait a minute! I've heard of this story." I looked at Dad and he nodded. "There are stories about a flood that covered the earth from almost every place in the world where people lived a long time ago."

"Hey!" Dr. Doone was surprised. "You know a lot about these flood stories. Where did you hear about them?"

I just smiled. Dad told him about our trip across the United States where we found clues left by Noah's Flood. Dr. Doone was very impressed. I was listening with one ear and kind of remembering the trip when I saw something moving across a sandy hill in the distance. I tried to watch closely to see exactly what it was, but the sun hurt my eyes. Whatever it was, it disappeared behind another hill.

"You know, Zack," Dr. Doone was saying, "when the Gilgamesh stories were first found, some people believed that the Bible story of Noah was copied from those adventures."

"But wasn't the story of Noah written first?"

Dad spoke up. "Think about it, Zack. Who wrote the

book of Genesis? Who wrote the story of the Flood?"

I knew that. The first five books of the Bible were all written by…"Moses."

"That's right," Dad agreed. "Now this story of Gilgamesh was an old story written on clay tablets collected by a king who lived in the days of Abraham. And Abraham was Joseph's great-grandfather. Remember that Joseph was the first Hebrew to settle in Egypt. Five hundred years went by before Moses was born. Look at your string again."

That's right, I thought to myself. The pink knot is for Moses' time. "Wow. Gilgamesh's story was written a long time before Genesis. How do we know Moses didn't just copy Gilgamesh's story and call the hero Noah instead?"

Dr. Doone started to answer, but I jumped up and pointed to the hill in front of us. "What's that?"

The only thing I could see was a head coming over the top of the hill. The sun was still in my eyes but it was either the ugliest person I had ever seen or it was…"A camel!" I called out to Dad. "It's a camel and someone is riding it."

The camel stepped slowly down the hill toward us. The man riding it wore a long, flowing robe like Sheik

Hamadi. He sat high up on the hump and rocked forward and back, forward and back as the camel stepped. He stopped in front of the car and spoke in a friendly voice.

"You are...troubled? Your car is thirsty for gas?"

He didn't speak English very well, but it was clear he wanted to help us. Dr. Doone tried to explain that the car was broken and that the driver was gone to the next village to get another car. It was hard to make the man understand.

"I will take you on my camel," he said. I laughed at the idea of Dr. Doone riding on a camel. Then I realized that the man was talking to me!

"You do want to ride a camel, don't you, Zack?" Dr. Doone asked with a grin. "He wants you to ride with him to find some gas."

"But we didn't run out of gas. We don't need any gas," I said. I wasn't so sure I wanted to get up on that camel. It looked taller than my basketball goal.

Was I ever glad when our driver popped over the hill in a new car. He was able to explain the problem to our camel-riding friend and started moving our stuff to the new car. I patted the camel's hairy knee, waved to the man on top and quickly slid into the cool, air-conditioned car.

Later that night at the tent, Dr. Doone answered my question about the Flood story.

"The story Gilgamesh wrote is a lot like the Bible story about Noah. But in many ways, it is very different. In Gilgamesh's story, the earth is flooded because some of the gods above the earth are fighting with each other. The hero is saved because he is clever enough to build a boat, not because he is faithful to God."

I thought about that. "So the difference is that Gilgamesh's story has the wrong god."

"I think that the story of the Flood was told by fathers to their children for many, many years. But wherever people turned away from God, they twisted the Flood story so that the true God wasn't in it anymore."

That made me laugh. I mean, it's funny if you think about it. I can just imagine a father telling his children about the real story of the Flood and then saying, "But we don't follow that God anymore." Kids aren't dumb. They would say, "You must be crazy! A God that can flood the whole world? We need to find out about him."

Dad just came by and told me to get to sleep. We have to get up early tomorrow, he said. We're leaving at sunrise to search for Sodom and Gomorrah! I wonder if there will be anything left to find. I thought it all burned up.

The sheik's daughter, Hallah, just waved to me again. Good thing we're leaving. I don't want to hang around long enough for the sheik or his daughter to get any more ideas.

Discoveries and Clues

Words to Remember

Cuneiform: Triangular-shaped writing used by people around Babylon and Ur in Abraham's time

Gilgamesh: An ancient storyteller

Important Facts

Gilgamesh's story was written long before Bible. It tells about a flood like the Bible story, but it has the wrong god and reasons for the flood are twisted.

FIVE

Friends that Rhyme

Selfish Sea

Dad had a nice surprise for me this morning. When I got outside to help load up the car, he introduced me to our new guide, Mr. Hasseim. Then he told me the good news.

"Zack, you'll be happy to know that Mr. Hasseim's son will be coming with us. He's about your age and his name is Achmed (ock-med). I've already told him about you."

The kid stepped out from behind the car and put out his hand to shake. "I am very happy to meet you, Zock," he said carefully. I shook his hand and smiled even though he said my name like it rhymed with sock.

"I'm glad to meet you, Achmed," I said.

"I am very happy you can talk to me," he said. "Now I can learn English better." This time I laughed out loud.

"You wouldn't say that if you had seen my grades in English last year," I said. Dad had to laugh at that one.

"What would I say?" he asked, kind of confused. "You are speaking English, yes?"

"Yes. And I will be happy to help you learn to talk like I do. But I'm not sure that it will be good English. Your name is Achmed? Can I just call you 'Ach'?"

He liked that idea. "Our names sound the same— Zock and Ach."

We all hopped in the car and headed out across the dry hills. I asked Ach if he liked baseball. He didn't know what baseball was! Can you believe that? So I tried to explain it to him. I told him there were nine players on each team. I told him that the team that was batting tried to score runs and the team that was out in the field was trying to stop them.

"The team batting must run to score?" Ach asked.

"That's right," I said. "Unless the pitcher walks in a run."

Ach was confused. "The pitcher must walk to score? That doesn't seem fair if the others can run."

"No, no," I said. "If the pitcher walks, the other team scores. The pitcher doesn't want to walk anyone."

"I wouldn't want to walk either if everyone else could run," he said.

I groaned. Dad laughed. "Maybe you'd better start over."

Luckily, just then Dr. Doone asked Mr. Hasseim to stop at the top of one hill and everyone got out. "This is the middle of nowhere," I said. "Why are we stopping here? I don't see anything interesting."

"This is where we film first today," Dad said. "Help me get the camera out and set up."

"Okay. Let's go, Ach."

Dr. Doone stood at the top of the hill. We stayed back as Dad focused the camera. We could see a long way in all directions. Behind Dr. Doone, the sunlight was reflecting off something and flashed in my eyes.

"What's that?" I started to ask.

"Shhh," Dad whispered at me. "Okay, Dr. Doone. Whenever you're ready." He had the camera in place.

Dr. Doone coughed and cleared his throat. "Okay, let's start." And then he began his talk.

"On one of the hilltops near here, Abraham and Lot stood together to make an important decision. Their flocks were growing and their shepherds were fighting. Lot and Abraham had lived together for many years, but it was time to separate. Abraham, the leader of the family, should have chosen the land he wanted and left the rest for Lot. But Abraham was not a selfish man. He let Lot choose."

I tried to whisper my question to Ach. "What's out there that's so shiny?" He looked confused, so I tried again. "Out there," I said, pointing towards it. He squinted his eyes and tried to see what I was pointing at.

"Shhh!"

I gave up and listened to Dr. Doone again.

"In those days, this land was not all desert and sand. The cities of the plains were surrounded by beautiful green fields and cool running water. It was a perfect place for someone with many sheep. When Abraham let Lot decide, Lot took the rich land near the cities. But it turned out to be a bad choice. At our next stop, we'll search for the cities of the plains, for Sodom and Gomorrah."

As soon as the camera was off, I ran up the hill and looked for whatever was shining out there. A cloud moved over the sun and I could see clearly. It was water! Lots of water! But something looked wrong.

Dr. Doone and Ach came up behind me. "Dr. Doone," I said, "look at all that water down there. Why isn't there any green grass or trees? I know it's hot, but things should still grow with that much water around. There's just white sand and rocks around the water."

Dr. Doone shaded his eyes and looked out over the

water. "Achmed, why don't you tell him."

Ach looked at me. "It is called the Dead Sea. Nothing can grow from its water. The water kills things that are green."

I looked up at Dr. Doone. "Why does the water kill things?"

"For good reason, Zack. But that's where we are going next, so I'll explain when we get there."

On the way, I remembered the question I was going to ask Dr. Doone. "Dr. Doone, what are those small hills we sometimes see along the road?"

"Believe it or not, those hills are old cities. We call them tells. Over the long years, those cities were destroyed or abandoned. They were slowly covered up by the desert."

We bumped down to the edge of the Dead Sea. Then Dad set up the camera again and Dr. Doone started another speech. Ach and I walked down to the water. I wanted to see the white rocks and sand. I kicked at one rock and it broke apart. I tried to kick up some sand but it wasn't loose like sand.

"Hey, what is this stuff?"

Ach bent down and grabbed a white rock. Then he crumbled it in his fingers. "It is salt." He put some on his tongue. "See?"

I put a tiny bit on my finger and licked it. "You're right. It is salt." I saw Dr. Doone walking toward us. "Hey, now I know why nothing grows here," I shouted. "Because it's salt water, like the water in the ocean."

I knew about salt water in the ocean. One summer we went to the ocean to camp and swim. I cut my big toe on a seashell when we were walking down to the beach. So I hopped over to the water to wash it off. Ouch! Was that ever a mistake! Boy, did it sting when the salt water got into it. And I do know that nothing grows in the salt water of the beach except some seaweed. But one thing I still didn't understand.

"Why is it salty? This isn't the ocean."

"The Dead Sea is salty because it's selfish," Dr. Doone said.

"What?" I looked at Ach. He shook his head. He didn't understand either.

"A very small amount of salt is in the water that comes into the Dead Sea from the Jordan River. But when the water gets here, it just sits. It doesn't flow out. There are no rivers or streams that leave the Dead Sea. It's trapped. As the water slowly dries up in this hot sun, it leaves the salt behind."

"So what makes the Dead Sea selfish?"

"It's kind of like us when we are selfish. It takes from

others, but never gives anything to anyone. If we are self-ish like that, we'll have about as many friends as the Dead Sea has plants. None."

I could understand that. I know some kids who are selfish, only worried about what they want and not any-one else. I don't like to be around them. We walked back to where Dad was waiting at the car.

"Hey, Dr. Doone. What about Sodom? I thought we were here to find the old city that burned up," I asked as we walked.

"What? Oh, that's right. You and Achmed were down here while I was talking about Sodom." He stopped and pointed back to the water. "Zack, for a long time, most archeologists believed that Sodom was out there some-where, that the sea had covered it up. But not long ago, some archeologists began digging at some old city sites near here along the shores of the Dead Sea. They have found evidence that one of those sites might be Sodom."

"Great! Let's go see it."

By now we were at the car. Dad was listening to what we said and he had something to say.

"Hey, not so fast. We're camping here tonight. Let's go ahead and set up camp. Then we can go on exploring. We have other things to see today. We'll see those places tomorrow. What do you think about the Dead Sea, Zack?"

"I think they should have named it the Selfish Sea," I said.

"What?"

I looked at Ach and we both laughed. "I'll explain later, Dad. Come on, Ach. Let's get the tents out and set them up."

With Ach helping, the tents went up fast. We stopped for a drink of water. "Do you like camping in my country, Zock?" Ach asked.

"Oh, yeah," I said. " I think it's pretty cool."

He looked confused again. He wiped sweat off his head and said, "That's funny. I thought it was pretty hot."

I can see I have lots of things to explain to Ach.

Discoveries and Clues

Words to Remember

Achmed: I like him, even if he doesn't know anything about baseball.

Dead Sea: What happens when water flows in but doesn't flow out

Tells: Small hills hiding the sites of old cities—good places to dig for artifacts

Important Facts

Even a sea can be selfish if it always takes from others and never gives. And just like the Dead Sea, selfish people aren't fun to be around.

Danger in the Dust

Better than Baseball?

A lot of stuff happened today. I'm really not sure I have time to write it all down. I'll write now as we bounce along, and if I don't get to finish now, I'll get caught up tomorrow.

While we ate breakfast, I tried to explain baseball to Ach again. "One team is out on the field, trying to catch the ball. The other team is in, trying to hit the ball. One player stands at the plate and..."

"The plate? Oh, the team that is in gets to eat."

"No, no. Home plate." I put my hand to my head. "It's just what they call the base where you stand to hit the ball. Now the pitcher throws the ball to the catcher. And the batter..."

"Wait," Ach said. "Who is this catcher?"

I took a deep breath. "The catcher is the player who

sits behind the plate to catch the ball."

"Do not all the players try to catch the ball?"

"Yes, when someone hits it or throws it to them."

"Then they are all catchers, right?"

"Yes, but…Dad, help me, please." I looked over at him but he was no help. He almost choked on his food he was laughing so hard.

"Sorry, buddy. You're on your own. Good luck."

Luckily for me, it was time to load up and leave. I was beginning to wonder if I could ever make Ach understand baseball.

When we stopped at the site of an old city, a lot of people were already there, stirring up small clouds of dust. Dr. Doone went over to talk to them while we got the camera set up. He came back soon and told us he was ready to film.

"Some people doubted that Sodom ever really existed. Then archeologists discovered the name of the city on a clay tablet from Sodom's time period. So the search for Sodom began. While many feel that the city is under the waters of the Dead Sea, others believe this may be the site of Lot's home town. Archeologists digging here uncovered a clay tablet in this spot." Dr. Doone pointed down into a ditch about three feet deep. "On it they found the name of the king of Sodom, the same name the Bible gives as the king of Sodom in Lot's time.

"In this ditch, you can see part of a layer of ash that is five feet thick. This type of layer has often been found when cities were destroyed by a volcano. But," Dr. Doone smiled mysteriously, "there are no volcanoes in this area. How can it be explained? The Bible story fits the archeological clues exactly."

Achmed and I wandered over to watch the people working. We had to walk carefully because there were strings crisscrossing the whole area. I thought the workers would be digging with shovels but most of them were using small brooms and brushes. Dad and Dr. Doone walked up behind us so I asked, "Why are they using brushes to dig?"

"Zack, remember how old these cities are. Most of what was here has rotted away and turned back into dirt. We may find some broken pieces of pottery or clay tablets or some little bits of silver or gold jewelry. Whatever is here, we don't want to break it. So we have to dig very carefully."

Ach asked a question. "Why are all these strings here? Is this another American game?"

"No, Achmed. The archeologists use the strings to make the site into little squares. That way they keep track of exactly where every little thing is found," Dr. Doone explained. "It helps them see how the old city might have looked."

"They must have a good imagination," I marvelled. "I wouldn't have guessed in a million years that a city ever was here."

Dr. Doone nodded his head. "The ditch helps them get a picture of the old city, too. At many of these old city sites, there was more than one city. When you dig down, you find that one city is built on top of the wreck of the city before it."

"I don't understand," I said.

"Think of the story Jesus told about the good Samaritan. Do you remember where the man who was robbed was going?"

I couldn't remember. But Dad could. "He was on the road to Jericho."

"That's right. But what do we know about Jericho in the time of Joshua?"

I knew this one. I had heard the story many time. "It was destroyed. The walls came tumbling down and all the people were killed. So why is there a city called Jericho in Jesus' days?"

Dr. Doone smiled. "That is exactly what I'm trying to tell you. If we went to the hill of Jericho today, we could dig down and find clay pottery and tablets from the Jericho in Jesus' time. And if we kept digging down, we could find things from the Jericho of Joshua's time. It's all right here."

"All in the same place?"

"Yes. Remember that more than one thousand years went by between Joshua's time and Jesus' time. When the new Jericho was built, there were no signs of the old one. But it was still a good place to build a city. It was on a hill, easy to defend against enemies, and it had a good fresh water supply. People even rebuilt on the site of the city of Sodom here after it burned."

This archeology is harder than I thought. I was going to ask if we could help dig or brush or something, but Dr. Doone started explaining about the ditch.

"A ditch like this helps the archeologists by showing the layers of the site. Then they can see where an old city ended and where a new one begins."

We looked at the ditch for a few minutes and then Ach beat me to the question. "Dr. Doone," he asked, "can Zock and I dig and look for artifacts?"

"I'm sure the workers here would be happy for your help. But you'll have to be very careful."

The workers gave us some brushes and buckets and another warning to be careful. Dr. Doone took us to our spot in one little square at the corner of the city. He gave us a few more hints about finding artifacts.

"Brush the dust and dirt away carefully. Put any rocks in the buckets. Don't throw them away. Sometimes good pieces of pottery look like rocks. If you see anything that isn't dirt or a rock, don't try to pick it up. Just brush around it and call me. Have fun."

At first, it was great fun. I really made the dust fly! A gust of wind carried a cloud of it right over to Ach. He covered his eyes and coughed.

"Sorry, Ach. Are you finding anything?"

"Oh, yes!" he said.

I jumped up and ran over to his spot. "What? What did you find?"

"I found five rocks already. They are in my bucket."

"Oh, Ach." I worked hard for a few minutes and I discovered something. I discovered that being an archeologist is hard work. And hot. All that dust was starting to choke me. I found a few rocks, but nothing interesting.

"This isn't as much fun as I thought it would be," I said to Ach.

"Is baseball more fun than this?" he asked.

"You'd better believe it." I jumped up and swung an imaginary bat. "We'd be hitting the ball and catching it and sliding into home and—"

Ach broke in. "Would all the running and hitting make you hot?"

"Yes."

"And all the catching and sliding would make you dusty?"

"Well, yes."

"Are you not already hot and dusty here? Why isn't this the same as baseball?"

I sighed and shook my head. "Ach, I still have a lot to teach you."

We worked for a while and my back was starting to hurt, so I stretched out on the ground and dusted lying down. "Much better," I said to Ach. "Now I can rest while I work."

"Zock," Ach said in a strange voice, "please do not move."

I looked over at him. "What?" I asked. His eyes were as big as baseballs and they were staring at my feet. I glanced down there, trying to figure out what his problem was. I figured it out, all right. But it wasn't his problem. It was mine!

Now that I was stretched out, my feet were right beside a big, fat, coiled snake!

Discoveries and Clues

Words to Remember

Help!

Important Facts

People doubted that Sodom was real, but it is mentioned on clay tablets from that time. Now archeologists think they have found the site of Sodom.

The site they think is Sodom has a layer of ash five feet thick. With no nearby volcanoes, it had to be caused by fire from somewhere else (God).

People in Bible days often rebuilt cities on the same site that old cities had been. This leaves layers of artifacts from each time that the city was lived in.

Archeologists dig with brushes, not shovels.

SEVEN

Buried Treasure

Achmed Rocks!

The snake waved its head from side to side, like it was looking for the best place to bite. I was ready to jump up and run but when I looked at Ach, he shook his head.

"No. Be very still," he said. "This snake bites quickly." He held up his left hand like a policeman stopping traffic. Reaching slowly into his bucket, he pulled out a rock. "When I count to three, roll away from it."

I held my breath. The snake flicked its tongue.

"One." Ach raised his arm.

"Two." He whipped his hand down and the rock flew.

"Three!" I rolled away as the rock zipped by. It just nicked my leg and then hit the snake right on the head. I jumped up onto my feet beside Ach. The snake slumped back and uncoiled very slowly.

Ach grabbed a basketball-sized rock and dropped it on the snake's head. "He will not be so fast now," he said.

I grabbed his arm. "Ach, you were great! You saved me. Where did you learn to throw like that?"

67

He kind of grinned and scuffed his foot in the dirt. "We don't always have a game to play at my school. We don't have a baseball. But always, we have rocks. So we throw many rocks. I am the best thrower at my school."

"You would love baseball. You'd be a great pitcher."

Ach kind of frowned. "I'd rather be a thrower."

"But that's what..." I started to try to explain, but Dad showed up.

"Hey, what's going on? Didn't they tell you not to throw the rocks?"

I didn't say anything. I just pointed at the snake's tail. The part that stuck out from under the rock was still wiggling just a little.

"Wow," he said. "Good thinking. Is it dead?"

"We think so. Ach hit it on the head with a throw that would have been a great fastball. Then he dropped this monster rock on him." I patted Ach on the back. "He's got a great arm."

Dad patted Ach on the back too. "Thanks, Achmed. I'm really glad you're with us."

He helped us look to see if any of the snake's relatives were around and then left us to our digging. We had stirred up a lot of dust and rocks when Ach thought he found something.

"Zock, look quickly. It is hard, but it is not a rock." I helped him brush away more of the dirt. "See, it is round."

"Like maybe a bowl or a dish," I said. "I'll get

Dr. Doone." I jumped up and shouted, "Dr. Doone! Dad! Come and see what we found."

They both ran over to me. "What is it, Zack?" Dad asked. "Not another snake, I hope."

"No, it looks like a piece of pottery. Come and see it. Ach dug it up. I mean, brushed it up. No…well, you know what I mean."

By this time, we were back at Ach's spot, and Dr. Doone bent down to look more closely. "I think you boys are right. It's a piece of pottery. Let's let the archeologists here dig it out."

To make a long story short—and believe me, it was long—they did dig up the pottery. The archeologist and his helpers brushed it loose, bit by bit. It took more than an hour. It turned out to be the top half of a water vase. Dr. Doone says it was from around the time Jesus was on earth.

"How do you know that?" I asked.

"One of the ways archeologists tell the age of an old city like this is by the artifacts found there. We know that this type of water vase, with the long skinny neck like this, was made during the time of the Roman empire. And you'll remember that the Bible says that Roman soldiers were there when Jesus died."

"So if this was part of the Sodom when it was destroyed by fire, the vase would look different?"

"Oh, yes," he said. "Pottery from those times has

been uncovered here before. It's bigger around and not as tall. And the outside is not like this one. It's rougher."

I looked carefully at the broken water vase. It was hard to believe that someone long ago really poured a drink from it. Maybe even a kid like me. Did that boy grow up here in this place? Was he a shepherd like Sheik Hamadi or a fisherman like the disciple Peter? Maybe he was a soldier and fought against the enemy who destroyed his city. At some time, the water vase was either knocked over or thrown down and broken. Or maybe the wall fell in on top of it when the city was being captured and destroyed by an army.

"I wonder how it got broken," I said out loud.

Dad looked at me. "If this was anything like my house, it was probably knocked over at the dinner table by some boy who was in a hurry to eat."

I'm sure I don't know what he was talking about. I haven't broken any dishes since…well, not in a long time.

By then it was time to go, so I didn't discover any treasures or even any broken bowls. But I'm glad Ach did.

I'm sure Ach's dad was driving as carefully as possible, but that must have been the bumpiest road ever built. I kept checking my teeth to see if they were coming loose.

"Zock," Ach asked while he bounced from the seat to the ceiling, "tell me more about baseball. The pitcher must throw the ball to the catcher behind the—what did you call it—the bowl?"

"Behind the plate. The catcher is behind the plate. When the pitcher throws the ball, the person with the bat tries to hit it." I knew what he would ask next, so I explained, "The bat is a big stick."

"I understand now," Ach said. "But what if the catcher catches it before the person with the big stick can hit it?"

"The catcher doesn't try to catch it until after the batter swings at it. Unless it's a ball. Then the batter probably wouldn't swing."

"What else could it be? It has to be a ball. That is what the pitcher threw!"

I tried to groan. Dad started laughing again. I would have stuck my tongue out at him, but I was afraid we'd hit a big bump and my teeth would bite it off.

"Ach, the pitcher must throw the ball over the plate so that the batter has a fair chance to hit it. If his pitch goes over the plate in the right place, that pitch is called a strike. If it doesn't goes over the plate in the right place, then the pitch is called a ball."

Ach just looked at me with a blank face.

I tried again. "The pitcher always pitches the baseball. It's always a baseball. But it's either called a good pitch or a bad pitch. Good pitches are called 'strikes.' Bad pitches are called 'balls.'"

"Who names these pitches strikes and balls?"

"The umpire behind the plate."

Now Ach was really confused. "I thought you said

the catcher was the one behind the plate."

"The catcher is behind the plate. The umpire is behind the catcher. He is the one who decides if the pitch is in the right place over the plate."

Ach just shook his head. "Your baseball is very confusing. I think throwing rocks is better."

Just then I hit on a great idea. "What you need is to see a baseball game. Dad, will you play a little baseball with us tomorrow morning? I think Ach will understand it if he can see it. We could use the tennis ball I brought and a stick or something."

"Sure we could, Zack," he said, "but Ach won't be here tomorrow. Someone else will be driving us. Mr. Hasseim has to go home to his other job."

I looked at Ach. He must have felt like I did because his face looked kind of upset. I scooted over next to Dad.

"Dad, why can't Ach stay with us tomorrow even if his dad doesn't? Couldn't we take him to his home later this week?"

"I think it's a great idea, Zack, but remember, Dr. Doone is in charge of this trip. You'll have to ask him. And don't forget, someone has to ask Achmed's dad."

I told Ach about my idea, and he thought it was great. Since I didn't want to have to shout at Dr. Doone over the noise of the rattling window to ask him, I decided to wait until we stopped.

We stopped a lot sooner than anyone expected.

Discoveries and Clues

Words to Remember

Ball: A ball isn't always a ball. Sometimes it's a strike. Sometimes people can understand what you say without knowing what you mean.

Important Facts

Artifacts like water vases help archeologists tell when people lived in that city. Pottery looked different during Abraham's days than it did in Jesus' days.

EIGHT

Abraham's Picnic

Traffic Jam

Just when I finished talking to Ach, his dad slammed on the brakes and the car started sliding toward the right edge of the road. Good thing we had our seat belts on. I looked up to see what the problem was, and boy, did I see it! There was a flood of sheep coming down the road right at us!

There was no way around them. They filled the road from one side to the other. Mr. Hasseim twisted the steering wheel again and we slid to a stop in the middle of the road.

The sheep weren't hurt, but they were scared. They all started bleating and tried to turn and run. But their shepherds were behind them, shouting and waving their big sticks. By the time the dust settled, sheep were moving by on both sides of the car.

"Hey, Dad," I said, "this is the first time I've ever

seen a sheep traffic jam."

He laughed and looked out on his side. "That's right, it's bumper to bumper sheep out there."

Ach looked at him, then turned and looked at me. Dad and I burst out laughing. "Like cars, Ach. You know, in the city, when cars are crowded on the street and they are almost touching each other and every one is in a hurry."

He looked out at the sheep, then he started laughing too. His dad looked back at him and said something in their language. I couldn't understand Ach's answer either.

"Achmed is explaining what was funny to his dad," Dr. Doone said. "They're speaking a language called Arabic."

Ach's dad listened and then did the same thing Ach did. He looked out at the sheep and then laughed. But then he said something else to Ach. Ach started laughing even harder.

"What? What's so funny?"

Ach tried to stop laughing and tell me. "He said the sheep have no horns."

I looked at him, then turned and looked at his dad. I didn't understand. "Of course they don't have horns. They're not cows. They're sheep."

Ach said, "No, not horns. Horns. You know—beep beep."

Finally, I got it. He was right. The only thing missing from the sheep traffic jam was honking horns. Everyone was laughing now, so it seemed like a good time to bring up my idea.

"Dr. Doone, can Ach stay with us when his dad leaves tomorrow?"

He turned around and looked at me and Ach. I think he was surprised. "Well, you have both been a big help to us. And it's always good to have someone else along who speaks Arabic."

"And don't forget about the snake. He knew just what to do," I added.

"Achmed, do you want to travel with us?"

"Yes, Dr. Doone. I am learning many things."

He nodded. "I'll talk to both of your fathers and see if we can work something out."

Soon the sheep jam was past and we drove on to our next site. When we stopped again, Dr. Doone said, "Zack, where does the Bible say Abraham buried Sarah when she died? Look in Genesis 23:17–20."

I dug down in my duffel bag and grabbed my Bible. I got out my notebook, too. "It says that Abraham bought a field with a cave in it near Mamre (mom-ray)."

"That's right. And not only Sarah was buried in that cave. Abraham was, and so was Isaac and Rebekah, and Jacob and Leah. And," he said with a wave of his arm, "this is Mamre."

"Really? Is the cave here? Are we going to see it?" I asked.

"Whoa, Zack. The cave really is here, but we won't get to see it. This place is a...well, I'll be explaining it for the video in just a minute. Help your dad with the camera and things and then listen closely. After we finish, I have a surprise for you."

Ach and I hauled out the boxes with the camera batteries and cables and Dad set up the camera. Dr. Doone found his place in front of a strange-looking building surrounded by trees.

"Abraham was a stranger in this land. His flocks wandered the hills of Canaan and even though he was a rich man, Abraham wandered too. He and his tents moved from place to place when necessary and there was no city or village that he called home. When his wife, Sarah, died, he owned no land where she could be buried."

"In those days, caves were often used as cemeteries. Abraham bought a burial cave for his family from Ephron (ef-ron) the Hittite (hit-tight). That cave is here, at

Mamre. Abraham and Sarah are buried here, and so are Isaac and Rebekah and Jacob and Leah."

I looked over at Ach. "Let's go look at that building," I whispered, pointing behind Dr. Doone.

Ach's eyes opened very wide. He shook his head and whispered, "Listen."

"...and so Abraham is honored by the Arabic Moslem people also. The cave was sealed closed and to mark his burial place, this shrine was built over the site. So even though we can't go into the cave, we can see that this is evidence that the Bible story really happened, just like it says."

"Wow," I said. "What's a shrine?"

Ach answered in a whisper. "A shrine is a holy place. Like a church. But there are no meetings there."

After Dr. Doone was through, we packed it all up. "Now for your surprise," he said as we rolled away. But he wouldn't say any more until we stopped near a big oak tree.

"Come on, boys," he said. We all followed him, even Dad. I guess we looked like baby ducks following their mother. He led us over into the shade of the tree and then he stopped and sat down.

I looked at Dad. He just shrugged his shoulders and sat down too. I didn't understand what was going on, but I sat down with them. So did Ach. "This would be a nice place for a picnic," I said.

"I think Abraham would have agreed with you. Imagine that you are sitting here, with your tent spread out over there," Dr. Doone said, with a wave of his hand, "and your camels tied up there. Then, off in the distance, you see three people walking toward you. Soon you can see that they are strangers and you walk out to meet them. They come back and sit here with you and you find out that they are angels and they are going to Sodom to destroy it."

I was almost imagining it. "Abraham was really talking to angels and to God in that story."

"That's right, Zack. And it all happened right here."

I jumped up. "What? Are you telling me that Abraham had a picnic with those angels under this tree? Right here?"

"Many people think that this is the same tree. Some archeologists think it probably happened at a site a few miles from here. But it's kind of exciting to think this might be the same spot," Dr. Doone said.

I'll say it was exciting! I walked around for a minute and tried to imagine Abraham and the angels being right there. And maybe God too! I'm glad I had my notebook along. I sat down and started writing. Ach came over and watched me.

"Hey, Detective Zack, since you're writing down evidence, I've got another clue for you," Dad said.

Ach looked at me with a question on his face. "What is a detective?" he asked.

"A detective solves a mystery. He finds clues and figures out what really happened. This is my detective hat," I said, lifting it up for a second, "and this is the notebook I write all my clues in."

"So that is what you are writing all the time. But what mystery are you solving?"

"Some people say that the stories in the Bible didn't really happen, that someone just made them up. I am trying to find out if the people in the Bible stories are real and if people really lived that way in those days."

Ach was thinking about that, so I asked Dad, "What clue do you have?"

He came and sat down. "Do you remember the name of the person that sold Abraham the cave? It was Ephron the Hittite. Dr. Doone was telling me that for many years, archeologists who weren't Christians pointed out that no one else in the world had ever heard of people called Hittites. That would mean that the Bible was wrong."

"That doesn't sound very good," I said.

"But then some more of those clay tablets with the

secret code writings were found and guess whose name was there—the Hittites. They were a strong nation of people who lived in Canaan about the same time that Abraham did."

"So the Bible turned out to be right again."

God is amazing! He had those tablets buried safely under the sand until we needed them. And you know what I think? I think when Abraham sat under this tree, he thought God was pretty amazing too!

Discoveries and Clues

Words to Remember

Arabic: A language spoken by Arab people (like Ach)

Shrine: A monument or holy place set up to honor a person or place

Important Facts

The Bible says that Abraham's family tomb is a cave near Mamre. It is still there today protected by a shrine.

There is a tree that may be the same one Abraham sat under. It's a very old tree.

People doubted that there were really any Hittites. But more clay tablets turned up and they talked about the Hittites just like the Bible did. The Bible is right again!

NINE

Old Beauty

I'd Rather Ride a Mountain Bike

Boy, is my seat sore! I never knew riding a camel could be so painful. Of course, I never knew anything about riding a camel—until today. And I didn't plan on learning about it today, but…well, it's a long story, so I'll start at the beginning.

First of all, the good news. Ach did get to stay with us. Dr. Doone told his father that we needed another helper and guide, so he agreed. Good thing too, because today we really needed Ach.

We started off in another taxi, looking for one of Abraham's wells. Dr. Doone wanted to do some filming there. It was a pretty normal day, if you can call all this driving around and camping out normal. In fact, Dr. Doone was telling us something very interesting. I had my notebook out to write down any clues about Bible times.

"Many people who didn't believe the Bible stories

were real said that the story of Abraham was just a legend. They said that life in those days wasn't like the Bible story."

"What evidence is there that the Bible story was true to life in Abraham's days?" I asked.

"Well, here's a good example. Do you remember that Abraham had no children for many years? And since God had promised to make his people a great nation, he was worried about who would be his heir (air)."

"What does 'heir' mean?" Ach asked.

"For Abraham, an heir would be the one who would take over the family flocks when he died. Someone who would lead the family, and teach them about God. Usually, the oldest son would be that person, but Abraham had no children."

"So who was going to be his heir?" I asked.

"You can find out by reading Genesis 15:2."

I dug into my duffel bag again and found the text in my Bible. "It says, 'the heir of my house is Eliezer of Damascus.' Who's that?"

Dr Doone answered. "Eliezer was Abraham's oldest and most trusted servant. He's the one whom Abraham sent to find a wife for Isaac later."

"Why was a servant the heir?" Ach asked.

"That's the really interesting part. Not too many

years ago, a family in Nuzi (new-zee), a city near Nineveh, was digging in their yard. Instead of just dirt, they dug up some clay tablets. When archeologists heard about it, they came and started digging more."

"But carefully," I said.

"Yes, carefully. What they found was amazing. Thousands of tablets, covered with the secret code writing, cuneiform, were dug up. Archeologists learned much more about life during the days the Bible says Abraham was alive. They read about customs that were exactly the same as those described in the book of Genesis."

I was writing as fast as I could in my notebook.

He went on. "And guess what those tablets said about a man who had no son to be the heir of his property? They said that he could adopt a trusted servant to be his heir."

"That's just what Abraham did," I said. "So the Bible story was true to life."

"It sure seems that way to me," Dr. Doone said. Just then, we heard a strange sound from the engine of the car. Then smoke or steam started pouring out from under the hood. "Oh, no," Dr. Doone said, "not again."

The driver stopped and got out to open the hood. We sat in the car until it was too hot and then we piled out onto the sand. "Any hope of getting it going again?"

Dad called to Dr. Doone, who was standing by the driver.

Ach went over and listened to their conversation. The driver walked back in the direction we came from. "He's going back to that last village. He thinks maybe he can find something to take us on to the next city."

"Well, that's good," Dad said. "Then we shouldn't have to wait too long."

"I hope not," Dr. Doone said, with a strange look at my dad. "He said that there weren't usually any bandits or robbers along this road during the daytime. I told him to bring the first thing he could find."

I looked at Ach. He nodded. "Does that mean we shouldn't worry?" I asked.

"It means we should worry," he said.

We did worry. And we sweated. When I saw Dad with his eyes closed and his lips moving, I knew he was praying about our problem. I closed my eyes and asked God to stay with us and keep us safe. I felt better, and this time we didn't wait very long. The driver was back with a ride for us. Only it wasn't what we were expecting.

I grabbed Ach by the arm. "Camels! What are we going to do with camels?"

Ach looked at me. "Ride them, of course."

"Well," Dr. Doone said, "I did tell him to bring the first thing he could find."

The driver hopped down and Dr. Doone and Ach went over to talk to him. Dad came over by me and we stared up at the three camels. "Well, this will be something to write home about. You always wanted to ride a camel, didn't you, Zack?"

"Right, Dad. Just like I always wanted to ride my mountain bike downhill with no brakes."

He laughed. "It can't be that bad. Think of it as a horse with a hump."

Dr. Doone told us the plan. "The driver wants to stay here with his car. He says we can take the camels across the hills on this path to the next city. Then we can get another driver and leave the camels with his cousin."

"We're taking the camels without a guide? That doesn't seem like a good idea," Dad said.

"Of course we have a guide," Dr. Doone said. "We have Achmed here. He's a camel expert."

Ach walked up, leading one of the camels. "Okay, expert," Dad said, "teach us the first lesson. How do we get on?"

"Like this," he said. Then he spoke to the camel and tapped its shoulder with a stick. The camel slowly bent down until its front knees were on the ground. Then Ach reached up and grabbed the hump and jumped on. "See?"

The camel stood up, but Ach spoke to it again and it

knelt back down. He hopped off. "Dr. Doone, you try this one." After only a few tries, Dr. Doone was on top and ready to go.

"Okay. You next," he said to Dad.

"No problem," Dad said. Then he hopped up on the next one like he grew up on a camel ranch.

Then it was my turn. "Zock, you will ride with me. We will ride Old Beauty here." Old Beauty, one of the ugliest camels in the world, knelt down in front of me.

"I think I need a ladder," I said, looking up at the camel's hump.

"I'll jump on first, then help you," Ach said. He hopped up and stuck his hand down to me. "Let's go."

I took a deep breath. "Okay." I grabbed his hand and jumped and suddenly I was on top of a camel.

We got directions again from the car driver and then turned the camels toward the hills. We rode slowly along, dipping forward and back, forward and back.

"How are you doing, Zack?" Dad called from his camel. "Would you still rather be riding a bike?"

I waved at him and smiled.

So now you know why my writing looks so strange. I've been using a camel's hump for a desk. Uh oh, we're stopping. And Ach looks worried. I hope that doesn't mean we're lost.

Discoveries and Clues

Words to Remember

Heir: The person who inherits or takes over everything owned by the one who died

Camel: A horse with a hump?

Important Facts

Tablets from Nuzi show that in Abraham's day, you could adopt a family servant to be your heir, exactly like Abraham did with Eliezer.

TEN

Three Sheep and a Bowl of Beans

Camelback Bride

This looks like trouble," Dr. Doone said from the top of his camel. "That driver didn't say anything about the path splitting here. Which way do you think we should go, Ach?"

Ach looked around. "From here, I cannot tell which is the right path. Zock and I will ride to the top of that hill and look. You can wait here."

"Wait a minute, Achmed," Dad said. "I'd like to get down and look around while you are gone."

Ach looked puzzled. "That is okay," he said.

"But how do you get down from a camel?"

I laughed so hard I nearly fell off my camel. "Dad, you don't get down from a camel. You get down from a duck!"

Ach looked at me like I was crazy. "Why would anyone get up on a duck?"

I tried to explain. "It's just a joke. Some people use duck feathers to make soft pillows. We call those feathers 'down.' So you can get down from a duck but not from a camel. See?"

"You're a funny guy, Zack," Dad said, but he didn't laugh. I guess it wasn't that funny.

Dad went on. "Anyway, Achmed, we don't know how to make the camels kneel down so we can get off."

Ach took our camel over beside Dad's. He spoke to it and gave it a tap with his stick. Dad's camel knelt down, but so did Old Beauty. I started sliding and grabbed her hump with both hands. "No, no, Beauty," Ach said and pulled up on her rope.

"Crazy camel," I said.

We got Dr. Doone down and went on toward the top of the hill. But from the top, we couldn't see any signs of the next city. We were headed slowly back down toward the path when I looked up and saw that Dad and Dr. Doone were surrounded by people on camels.

"Ach! Look at all those people. I wonder who they are?"

He looked a little worried. I felt worried. Could they be robbers? "Ach, see if Old Beauty here will slip into high speed. Let's get back there as quick as we can."

"Right," he agreed. He started talking to the camel and then he hit her three times on the side with his stick. Suddenly, I was busy trying to hold on.

"Hey, she actually has a fast speed," I shouted.

We pulled in among the other camels and stopped right beside Dad and Dr. Doone. "Achmed and Zack, we've found some friends. These men tell us to keep following the path to the left and we will find the city."

Soon we waved to the strangers and rode off to the left. "Who were those men, Dad?" I asked.

"It seems strange, but that was a wedding party."

"A wedding? They didn't look like they were going to a wedding."

"Well, Zack, they were not going to the wedding. Not yet, anyway. Tonight, they are going to get the bride."

"Wait a minute, Dad. They are going to get the bride? What about the man who's marrying her?"

He laughed. "I'm sure they have it all worked out. It's a lot like the story of Isaac and Rebekah. Remember, Abraham sent Eliezer to find a bride for Isaac. He found Rebekah, and brought her home to Isaac. This man's friends have gone to get his bride and bring her to him."

Well, I guess that's a good clue that the Bible story was real. Brides still get delivered on camelback today, just like in Isaac's day.

We found the city and the driver's cousin and got rid of Old Beauty and the other camels. We found another taxi driver that would take us on to the old well, but I think his car looked worse than the one that broke down this morning. Finally we got to the well and set up the camera and stuff.

"In the village of the Bible days," Dr. Doone began, "the well was the center of activity. Everyone had to get water for themselves and their animals, so everyone came to the well. There they told their stories and spread the latest news."

"Hey, Ach," I whispered, "the latest news is, I'm thirsty. I wonder if there is any water in that well now."

He covered his mouth to keep from laughing.

Dr. Doone went on. "Abraham's servant Eliezer found Rebekah at a village well like this one. She offered to draw water for his camels. Jacob met Rachel at the same well, when she was watering her father's flocks of sheep. This well was one of the wells of Abraham. He spent the last years of his life in this area. Isaac and Rebekah and Jacob and Esau must have spent many years near here also."

Later, when we were loading up to leave, Dr. Doone said, "Zack, I remembered another clue you might want to write in your notebook. Pull it out and I'll tell you after we get rolling."

In the car, I got out my notebook and handed Ach my Bible just in case. "Dr. Doone, I'm ready. Tell me the clue."

"You know the story of Jacob and Esau. You know that Esau was the oldest so he was supposed to get the birthright blessing."

I interrupted him. "I've never understood what that birthright thing was supposed to be."

"Okay, Zack. Let me see if I can explain. Today, when someone dies, the things they owned—their house and cars and money—are divided equally between the children. But if a person wants to, they can write out a will. A will is a legal notice that tells everyone that certain things go to certain people."

Dad broke in. "Like when your great-grandmother died, her will said to give your mother that painting on our living room wall at home."

Dr. Doone went on. "So with a will, a person can declare exactly what she wants done with the things she owns after she dies. A birthright was the same kind of thing in Bible days. The birthright blessing was usually given to the oldest son."

"That's why Esau was supposed to get it," I told Ach. He nodded.

"Abraham gave the birthright blessing to Isaac. That means that Isaac now owned all of Abraham's flocks and riches, and that Isaac was now the leader of the family. He was the pastor of the family too, and was expected to lead them in worshiping God."

I looked at Dad. After all, I'm the oldest son in his family. He just smiled.

"For Jacob and Esau, it was a problem. They both wanted it. Anyway," Dr. Doone said, "here's the clue. For many years, no one believed that the story of Jacob and Esau was true. Then, in those clay tablets found near

Nuzi, archeologists found that people in Abraham's days did buy and sell birthrights. One tablet told about a man who sold his birthright for three sheep."

"Wait a minute," I said. "Didn't someone sell their birthright in the Bible story?"

"They sure did. Look it up. It's near the end of Genesis 25."

Ach was already turning the pages. We read it together. "Esau," he said. "Esau sold his birthright for a bowl of bean stew and some bread."

"That is a good clue," I said. "Those clay tablets prove that the Bible stories are true to life. The people in the Bible really lived, just like it says."

My notebook is filling up fast.

Tonight, for once, we are staying in a hotel. I love camping out, but it is nice to take a shower once in a while. And to sleep on a soft bed. And there will be no sheep or goats or camels waking me up before I'm ready.

When I asked Dr. Doone where we are going tomorrow, he said to Dothan. When I asked what we would see, he laughed.

"We're going to see a well in Dothan," he said. "See if you can remember why a well in Dothan would be interesting."

I tried all during my shower to think of something, but I couldn't.

Discoveries and Clues

Words to Remember

Birthright: In Bible days, the oldest son had the right to keep most of the father's flocks or money when the father died. The birthright also made him the leader and pastor of the family.

Important Facts

Some Bedouin shepherds still go on camels to bring the bride to her wedding. It's a lot like Eliezer did when he brought Rebekah to Isaac.

The tablets from Nuzi tell us that it was legal to buy and sell birthrights. The Nuzi tablets tell us about a man who sold his birthright for three sheep. The Bible tells us that Esau sold his for a bowl of beans. The Bible shows what life really was like in those days.

ELEVEN

Deep Trouble

Deeper Trouble

Now, Ach, when a batter hits the ball and no one catches it, that's called a hit."

"I understand that one, Zock. When the ball is hit, it is a hit," he said.

I let out a deep breath. Finally, Ach was beginning to understand baseball. I was still hoping that Dad would play some baseball with us. Maybe tomorrow.

"If a batter hits the ball and someone catches it before it hits the ground, then the batter is out," I went on.

"Out of what?"

I groaned. "No, just out. He has to go back to the bench. When there are three outs, then the team batting goes out in the field to catch and the team out in the field come in to bat."

Ach smiled. "So the teams take turns. That is very nice."

"Now this is the good part," I said. "If a batter hits the ball over the fence and out of the ball park, that's called a home run."

"A home run. I see," Ach said. "He lost the ball and must run home because the other players are mad at him."

Slowly, I banged my head against the car window. "No, Ach. It's called a home run because the batter can run all the way around the bases back to home plate, where he started. It's a good thing. It makes everyone on his team happy, because they score a run."

"I hate to interrupt this class on baseball," Dr. Doone broke in with a laugh, "but it's time for a little archeology. We are almost to Dothan. Zack, did you ever remember what happened here?"

"No," I had to admit. I got out my notebook and Ach grabbed my Bible. "Okay, tell us."

"Look in Genesis 37:17," he said as we stopped. Everyone else hopped out, but Ach and I were busy flipping pages in the Bible.

"Here it is," I said. "So Joseph went after his brothers and found them near Dothan." We jumped out and ran after Dr. Doone. "It's about Joseph," we said.

He was standing by an open pit. "That's right. And what happened to Joseph here?" he asked.

We ran back to the car where the Bible was. "It says his brothers saw him and wanted to kill him," I read.

"Did they kill him here in Dothan?" Ach asked.

"No," I said, still reading, "they took his coat of many colors, and…so that's what we're doing here."

"What?" Ach asked. "Tell me."

"This is where…"

"Shhh!" Dad was behind the camera. "We're filming."

Dr. Doone began his talk. "Stories from this area tell us that this," he said, pointing to the pit, "is the dry well or pit that Joseph's brothers threw him into. Even if this isn't the exact one, Joseph must have been in one very much like it."

"Oh," Ach whispered. "Now I remember."

Dr. Doone went on. "Joseph was his father's favorite child, but his brothers hated him. Some wanted to kill him, but his oldest brother Reuben talked them into just throwing him into this dry well. Reuben hoped to come back later to rescue his little brother."

"Okay," Dad said, looking up from the camera. "That was good. Now we'll move in closer to the well."

"Come on," I said to Ach. We ran up to the edge of the well and looked in. "Ooooh, that's deep.

"And dark," Ach added.

Dr. Doone joined us. "Imagine what Joseph felt like. He wasn't much older than you two."

I tried to imagine. If I was down there at the bottom, could I climb out? I looked at the sides lined with stones. Maybe, if I had…

"Back up, Zack. We're ready," Dad called.

"Joseph knew that his brothers wanted to kill him," Dr. Doone began. "And he knew that if he was left at the bottom of the pit, he really would die. Remember that

Joseph was a favorite son. He probably got whatever he wanted at home. Suddenly, he was in deep trouble."

"Real deep," I whispered to Ach.

"Then Joseph heard his brothers calling his name. They had come back for him! They weren't leaving him to die after all. He must have been smiling when they pulled him to the top. But from the look in their eyes, he knew that his troubles weren't over. For a minute, he thought he was going home, but then they sold him for twenty pieces of silver. He was going to Egypt as a slave."

Later, Ach and I were looking down into the well again. I cupped my hands around my mouth. "Helloooo," I shouted. There wasn't any echo.

Ach dropped a rock. Clank, clank, clunk, it bounced off the sides and down to the bottom. "I'm glad I'm not down there," he said.

Dad and Dr. Doone joined us and we all sat at the edge of the well. "Joseph must have really been brave," I said.

Dad kind of laughed. "Joseph must have really been scared. He was probably hoping it was a bad dream. He must have hoped someone would wake him up. But you know what I think is the most amazing thing about Joseph?"

"What?" I asked.

"When all these bad things happened, he remembered God. Some people might have blamed God or said that God must not really care about them. But Joseph knew he was in big trouble and he knew that he needed God more than ever. So he decided to trust God no matter what happened."

I looked down in the well again. "I hope I can learn to trust God like that," I said. "Especially when I'm in deep trouble."

Dad put his arm around my shoulders. "You are learning that, Zack. Every day that you're a Christian, you're learning to trust him more."

"Hey, Zack," Dr. Doone said. "Here's something else for your notebook."

I pulled it out. "Only a few pages left. Okay, tell me."

"People have doubted the story of Joseph. After all, it's pretty amazing. But here's one clue that the story is real. Archeologists have found written records of slave selling and buying from different times. And the price of a slave has changed a lot."

I checked my notes. "Joseph was sold for twenty pieces of silver."

"That's right," he said. "In the days of Abraham, the price of a slave was around fifteen silver pieces. And by the time of Moses, it was close to thirty silver pieces. But during the days of Joseph, it was twenty pieces, just like the Bible says."

I wrote it all down as fast as I could.

Later I asked Dad, "Where do we go next?"

"We're following Joseph."

"You mean, we're going to Egypt?"

He laughed. "That's right. Tonight we go to the airport and we'll fly to Cairo, Egypt. Unless you'd rather ride there on Old Beauty."

I shuddered. "No. Airplane seats are more comfortable, thank you. Egypt will be great! I want to see the pyramids and the statues. And the crocodiles in the Nile River. But, Dad?"

"Yes?"

"What about Ach?"

"We'll drop him off at his home on our way to the airport. But don't worry. We're coming back in a few days. We'll find him again."

"But I told him we'd play a little baseball. He still wants to learn."

Dad thought about it. "We don't have time for a game, but I could hit you boys a few fly balls. You could show him how to catch."

"Come on, Ach," I shouted. "Dad's going to hit us some flies before we have to go."

"Oh, boy," Ach said. "But, Zock?"

"What?"

"Wouldn't it be more fun if he would hit the ball?"

It's a good thing we're coming back here. I still have a lot to teach Ach.

Discoveries and Clues

Words to Remember

Trust: Depending on God even when you're in deep trouble

Important Facts

According to clay tablets, the price of a slave in Joseph's day was twenty pieces of silver. That's exactly what the Bible says he was sold for.

TWELVE

A Really Big Watchdog?

Another Mystery

When Joseph came to Egypt as a slave," Dr. Doone explained to the camera, "this pyramid was already hundreds of years old. It was already famous as one of the wonders of the world. Taller than a forty-story building, this amazing structure is built completely out of blocks of stone."

Dr. Doone is right. It is amazing. Believe me, these are not little blocks of stone like bricks. They are all much bigger than I am. And you won't believe how many they stacked up to build it that tall. Dr. Doone says there are more than two and a half million blocks! And each one weighs more than a big car.

I asked him how the pyramid was built.

"No one really knows, Zack. Remember, they had to

cut each stone out of the quarry by hand. They didn't have dynamite. They had to move the stones all the way to the pyramid and they didn't have any trucks. They had to lift the stones up as the pyramid grew taller and they didn't have any cranes or helicopters. Somehow, they pulled, pushed, or carried those stones all the way to the top."

See? I told you it was amazing.

The next pyramid is guarded by the Sphinx (s-fink-s). I know you've seen lions carved out of stone before. The zoo in our town has one that I always used to climb on. Mom has pictures of all three of us kids sitting on the lion like it was a horse. When I was little, it seemed so big! Now, I can tell you that the zoo lion is a very small one, because I know what a big stone lion would look like.

Imagine a stone lion that would barely fit on a football field. Imagine that the same stone lion has the head of a man. Now imagine that the stone head has a nose that is five feet long and a mouth that is seven feet wide! Get the picture?

I was sitting in front of the Sphinx writing in my note-book when Dad came up to sit by me. "So what do you think, Zack?"

"I've got a question, Dad. Why? Why did they build these pyramids? Was this supposed to be a park or play-ground?"

"Dr. Doone was explaining that to me last night," he said. "The Egyptians were very religious people. They worshiped many gods. They believed that a person lived after death in some other place. And since they would be living, they needed their stuff. So they took it with them."

"Like what?"

"These pyramids are the burial grounds of kings. When they died, they wanted to take it all with them. They were buried with their gold and jewels. They took their chariots and spears and swords. This king here," he pointed to the biggest pyramid, "even had his boat buried with him."

"So these pyramids are all graveyards built big enough for all of a king's stuff. What about the Sphinx?"

"No one really knows. They think the face is supposed to be the king buried in the pyramid behind it. They think the Sphinx was supposed to guard the king's resting place."

"So he's really a big stone watchdog?"

He laughed. "A big stone watchdog. Or should we say a big stone watchsphinx? Anyway, he didn't do a very good job."

"What do you mean?"

"Robbers found a way to break into the king's tomb many, many years ago. All of his treasures were taken. In fact, all the pyramids of Egypt have been emptied by robbers."

People were crowding around us now, talking loud and taking pictures of the Sphinx and pyramids. I noticed a man in a red hat aiming a camera right at us. "Uh, Dad, I think we're going to be in someone's picture."

"Should we smile and wave or just get out of the way?"

"Come on, Dad. Let's go. Didn't I see a place where you could buy us something cold to drink?" I hinted.

We walked away and looked for the drink stand. Suddenly I noticed a strange smell that I almost remembered from somewhere. "Dad, do you smell . . ."

"Camel rides!" someone behind us shouted. "Camel rides around the pyramids."

I turned around to see five camels even uglier than Old Beauty. "Camel ride around the pyramid," a man said to me. "Only ten dollars. You ready?"

I laughed right out loud. Dad winked at me and said, "Come on, son. When was the last time you rode a camel?"

I turned to the man. "No, thank you. I'm just getting over being sore from the last time I rode a camel. I'm definitely not paying ten dollars to get sore again."

The man only smiled and said. "We have the softest camels. For you, only eight dollars."

I shook my head and walked away. And I had to elbow Dad to make him stop laughing.

Dr. Doone met us at the drink stand. We got our cold drinks and found a place to sit and watch the people coming to gawk at the pyramids. "Well, Zack, do you have your notebook?"

I whipped it out and flipped through the pages until I found the next blank page. "Yes, sir. Ready when you are."

He laughed and took a drink. "First of all, you should know that the Egyptians used a different form of writing. Their picture-writing or hieroglyphics (hi-row-glif-icks) have been found on the walls of temples and pyramids all over Egypt. But for many years, no one understood what it meant. No one could read it."

"So how did they break the secret code and read the pictures?"

"Some archeologists were looking at a stone marker that had been taken from Egypt and was in a museum. It had a lot of writing on it. They were excited when they realized that the message on the stone was written three times, in three different languages. One was written in Greek, which they could read, and another was hieroglyphics. So they read the Greek and used it to figure out the hieroglyphics."

I was impressed. "That was pretty good detective work."

"That stone is called the Rosetta Stone," he said. "It's

one of the most important things archeologists have ever discovered."

"So here in Egypt, we're looking for picture-writing." I made a note of that.

Dr Doone added, "And most of it will be carved in stone, instead of clay tablets."

I understood that. "Now give me a good clue about life in Joseph's days."

Dr. Doone took time for a drink before he started. "I mentioned that some thought the story of Joseph wasn't real-to-life. But archeologists have found evidence in Egypt that matches the Bible story exactly."

"Okay. Tell me what they found," I said.

"I already told you about the price of slaves being right for Joseph's time. Also, the titles or offices that are mentioned in the Bible fit with that time in Egypt," he said.

I wasn't sure I understood. "You mean like 'governor' or 'master' or something?"

"Right," Dr. Doone said. "You remember that Joseph was made the 'overseer' of Potiphar's house and later the overseer or prime minister of all of Egypt. This title for a person in charge has been found in other picture-writing of that time."

"So the name 'overseer' that was used in the Bible was used at that time in Egypt. What else?"

He laughed. "Slow down there, Zack. Do you remember the 'chief butler' and the 'chief baker' from Joseph's story?"

I thought for a minute. "Weren't they in prison with Joseph? And they had dreams like Pharaoh?"

"That's right. The titles 'chief butler' and 'chief baker' have been found in other writing from that time. Also, they found another person who had been the 'Keeper of the Royal Grain' like Joseph was during the years of famine. So you can see that the Bible story uses the same titles as the people of Egypt did during that time."

I was still writing when Dad said, "Let's find our way back to the hotel, Zack. I promised your mother that we would call home tonight. And some of us old people would like a little rest before tomorrow."

On the way back to the hotel, I heard a chicken squawk and turned around to see what was happening. The chicken was running away from a little girl, but I saw the same man in the red hat walking along behind us. When he saw me, he put his camera up like he was taking a picture.

I wonder if he's following us. Maybe he's just staying at the same hotel. But I wonder.

Discoveries and Clues

Words to Remember

Sphinx: A gigantic stone statue carved to look like a lion's body with a human head (It was supposed to guard its pyramid. It didn't do a very good job.)

Pyramids: Built to be safe burial places for the kings (This way, the kings could take all their valuable stuff with them.)

Hieroglyphics: Egyptian picture-writing carved in statues and monuments and stone walls all over Egypt

Rosetta Stone: The writing on this stone gave archeologists the clues they needed to figure out the picture writing.

Important Facts

Titles and offices mentioned in Joseph's story in the Bible are found in Egyptian picture-writing, too. Just what you would expect from a story that was true to real life.

THIRTEEN

Secrets in the Sand

Crocs in the Nile

Finally, I'm going to see some Nile crocodiles. Dad and I are on a river cruise that is supposed to show us some more temples and statues and some crocodiles. I know my brother Alex wishes he were here. When we called home last night, I got to talk to everyone. I told Alex about riding the camel.

"You're lucky," he said. "I wish I could ride one."

"Yeah, it's kind of fun," I told him. "But you sure do get sore fast. And when they run, you have to hold on to the hump with both hands."

Kayla asked, "Are the pyramids really cool?"

"Yeah," I said, "they're even bigger than I thought. The biggest one is a stack of more than two million blocks! And I've got this really cool friend over here. His name is Ach and he taught me about camels and throwing rocks. He doesn't know much about baseball, though."

I told her a little about the snake and she promised not to tell Mom about it. I guess Mom heard her because she brought it up as soon as she got on the phone.

"She promises not to tell me what? Zack, what's going on?"

"I'll tell you all about it as soon as I get home, Mom. Don't worry about me. I'm doing fine."

"What have you seen so far?" she asked next. "Did you find any good clues?"

I told her about Sheik Hamadi and Abraham's days and about Sodom (except the snake). I told her about the people going to a wedding on camels (I knew she'd like that mushy stuff), and about following Joseph to Egypt.

"Be careful. Be sure to brush your teeth and hurry home," she finally told me just before we said goodbye.

Dad joined me at the side of the boat. "Don't forget what the man said about keeping your arms and legs inside at all times."

"Don't worry. I want to see crocodiles, not be their lunch."

"Well, what do you think so far, Detective Zack?" Dad asked. "Are you finding enough clues to solve the mystery?"

"I think so," I said. "Whenever archeologists dig around here, they find things that agree with what the Bible says. We may not know too much about life that many years ago, but what we do know agrees with the Bible stories."

"So what does that mean?"

"It means that we could tell the lady at the airport that the Bible stories are real."

He leaned out and pointed. "Isn't that one of your crocodiles?"

It was a big one. And then I saw another one. And another. "This doesn't look like a good place to go swimming," I said.

Dad went on with our talk while we watched the crocs. "So what's the difference between the Bible stories and myths or legends?"

I had to think about that. "Myths and legends, like Santa Claus and the Tooth Fairy, are just stories. They may have started out about a real person, but now the story isn't real at all."

"And the Bible story?"

"The Bible is full of stories too, but they are about real life. People who lived in those days really did trade their birthrights, sell slaves, and fetch brides on camels. The Bible is about real people doing real things."

"So why does that matter?"

I tried to explain what it meant to me. "It's like when you tell me a story about something that happened when you were a kid. Knowing your story tells me that when you were a kid, you had problems just like me. And it tells me a good way to work on the problem. Either I can learn what to do or what not to do."

He smiled. "And the Bible does that too?"

"Yes. Because it tells me that Abraham and Jacob and Joseph were real people with real problems. And it tells me that God helped them with their problems. So I know he'll help me with mine too."

He pulled out the video camera and filmed the crocodiles for a few minutes. There were a lot of people on the boat taking pictures. Even that same man with the red hat.

Dad finally put the camera down. "Alex will like watching this. So what's the most important thing you've learned so far?"

"I'm not sure. Maybe what I learned from Joseph. That even if everything goes wrong and I'm in deep trouble, I can still trust God. Joseph did, and look how it worked out for him."

"That's great, Zack. You have learned something very important. But do you think if you told that lady in the airport all your facts, she would believe in God and be a Christian?"

I shook my head. "No, not really. But I'm not sure why. How come some people know all about the Bible but they still don't care about being a Christian?"

Dad kind of frowned. "It's a little like you and Achmed, Zack. You wanted him to know all about baseball. But even when he understood the words, he still didn't know what you were talking about. People can be that way about God. They can know all of the right words, know a lot about God, but still not know that Jesus can be a real friend."

"I guess you're right. Even some people who go to church seem that way." Someone threw a stick at the crocodiles. They didn't move an inch.

Dad sighed. "It's true. They don't understand being a Christian any more than Achmed understands baseball. They know the words, they even know the Bible, but they don't know Jesus."

I looked up at him. "And the best way to help them is to show them Jesus."

"Yes. Knowing that the people in the Bible were real is good, but be sure you know the most important person in the Bible, Zack. Make sure that Jesus is real to you, too."

Just then we heard a splash from behind the boat. I looked toward the sound for a second and when I looked back, the crocodiles were all gone. And I don't think they were running away.

I looked at the spot where they had been. "Crocodiles are scary to look at, but they may be even scarier when you know they are around, but you can't see them."

Dad agreed.

"Hey, I've got a good idea," I said to Dad as the boat left the crocodiles behind. "Why don't we mail my notebook home to Mom. Then they can see more of what we've been doing."

"She would love that, Zack."

"But what about the snake thing?"

"She'll be okay. Finish writing and we'll mail it when we get back to town."

I sat down here on a deck chair to finish. And this really is the last page. I'm glad the trip isn't over. There are some more mysteries I need to solve while we're here. Like, was Moses really almost a Pharaoh? Did the walls of Jericho really fall down? Was there really a lions' den for Daniel?

And what about that man with the red hat?

I still have a lot of things to teach Ach. And a lot of

things to learn from him.

I need a new notebook, but I'm keeping my old string with the knots. After all, we're almost up to Moses and his pink knot now.

I've changed my mind about the most important thing I've learned. I never thought there would be this much evidence about the Bible. I never imagined that you could dig in the sand and find out about things that happened so long ago.

I think that's the most important thing I've seen. I think that God covered those special artifacts with the sand and kept them secret until our days. And I think he did it just so people like me could be sure that he really is there and he really cares. About me.

I don't know for sure what Abraham or Isaac or Jacob or Joseph thought, but I think God is really amazing!

Discoveries and Clues

Important Facts

What archeologists have discovered about Bible times agrees with the stories in the Bible.

The Bible stories are about real people and real life. I know that if God loved them and helped them with their problems, he loves me and will help me, too.

Some people know all about the Bible, but they don't know Jesus. I can help them by showing them that Jesus can be a real friend.

The most important person in the Bible, Jesus, is real just like Abraham and Isaac and Jacob and Joseph.

God kept the secrets in the sand just for people like me. God really is amazing!

Faith
Building
Guide

Ages
9 and up

Trust

Secrets in the Sand

Spiritual Building Block: Trust

**You can learn how to trust God more and more
in the following ways:**

Think About It:

Remember back to a time when you felt like you were
in deep trouble because of what someone else did.
(Maybe you can relate to how Joseph felt at the bottom of a
well.) Were you furious with the person, looking for ways to
pay him back? Did you give in to sad feelings and give up
on hope? Did you ask God to help you make it through?
How would you do it differently now that the deep trouble
is over?

Talk About It.

Trusting God does not mean not caring anymore.
That's unrealistic. Find someone you respect to help
you deal with your feelings during your "deep-trouble"
times. Tell her why it's hard to trust God to help you

through this time. Ask her for stories, both biblical and present-day, that show God's care. Ask her to pray with you to know and to accept God's will.

Try It:

God is good and powerful. He loves you very much. During your next "deep-trouble" time, turn to God right away. Tell him honestly that you believe whatever he has planned for you is way better than whatever you could have planned for yourself (even though it doesn't seem that way). Spend as much time as possible praising him and thanking him for every single part of your life.

Detective Zack: Secret of Noah's Flood

"Nobody believes Noah and his Flood is a true story!" At least that's what Zack's friend Bobby says. What do you believe? Discover the truth about Noah's Flood in this action-packed story that will capture your imagination while it builds your faith in the Bible.

ISBN: 0-78143-730-X....................Retail Price: $5.99

Detective Zack: Mystery at Thunder Mountain

A "tribe" of unbelievers, strange cries in the night, large footprints in the canyon, and a series of thefts have Zack and Kayla searching for answers at Thunder Mountain Camp. Who is taking the horses out of the corral at night, and why? The list of suspects is growing longer every day. Everything is not what it seems at this summer camp.

ISBN: 0-78143-731-8....................Retail Price: $5.99

Detective Zack: Danger at Dinosaur Camp

Huge, unexplained footprints in the canyon, reports of a long-necked creature roaming the mountain, loud cries in the night! It can't be a living dinosaur—or can it? Could a dinosaur be at the bottom of all the strange happenings in Dinosaur National Monument? That's what Detective Zack is going to find out.

ISBN: 0-78143-732-6....................Retail Price: $5.99

Detective Zack: Missing Manger Mystery

Mrs. Hopkins warned that disaster was certain if the church Nativity scene were held outdoors. Truer words were never spoken! A fire nearly destroys the stable, and Mrs. Hopkinsí 80-year-old manger from Bethlehem is missing. Zack and his friend Luke chase the clues that eventually lead them to the villain and the true meaning of Christmas.

ISBN: 0-78143-803-9....................Retail Price: $5.99

Detective Zack: Red Hat Mystery

Zack's trip to the Middle East has taken a mysterious turn. Ever since the man in the red hat joined their tour group, things began to disappear. From Mt. Sinai to Jericho, to the valley where David fought Goliath, Zack and his friends try to stay one step ahead of a thief.

ISBN: 0-78143-802-0....................Retail Price: $5.99